MW01108327

For Two Cold Minutes

to Audrey, first, enjoy:
this was the first,

— [signature]

For Two Cold Minutes

Sarah J Dhue

Sarah J Dhue
2014

Copyright © 2012 by Sarah J Dhue

All rights reserved.

First Printing: 2012

ISBN 978-1-312-37311-2

Dedication

To my family, for their never ending
support and my friend Dree, for her help
and support

Social Network Profile

Robbie Pierce

About Me

Basic Info:	Sex:	Male
	Birthday:	October 8, 1992
	Parents:	Mariah Pierce
	Siblings:	Ryan Pierce
	In a Relationship with Lydia Farmer	

Bio: Name's Robbie, I came into this world October 8th 1992, so that would make me 17 going on 18. Here's some fun facts about me: favorite color is green, favorite animal is a rott weiler, favorite food is Coca Cola, I'm pretty obsessed with computer games, my favorite thing is Lydia Farmer ♥, my fantastic girlfriend (oh, by the way, I'm taken), hm... I play football, but not for school, for fun. I have a truck, I love it, it's awesome. It's also my best friend... JK, that would be Alex Newton and Sam West. There's not much else... I like art. And I have an awesome older bro named Ryan. *the end*

Likes and Interests

Activities:	football, art, school, Lydia >:]
Interests:	football, art, my truck, Lydia♥
Music:	Green Day, 3 Days Grace, Coldplay
Books:	Harry Potter
Movies:	X-men, Bourne, Spongebob
Television:	CSI, Spongebob, Scrubs, Psych

Contact Info
Email:	robpierce8@mail.com

September

September 1, 2010

Lydia laughed and swung her head to get her long blonde hair out of her eyes. The light of the streetlamp shined in her blue eyes, causing them to sparkle.

Robbie leaned across the car seat towards her, "Just one more," he said and she kissed him, grabbing his short brown hair and pulling him closer to her. They were beginning to make out when they saw the door of Lydia's house open and Robbie flew back to his side of the car like a rubber band being snapped.

"Well," he said, blushing, "Tonight was fun... or at least, I had fun."

"I did too," Lydia said, looking deep into his pale gray eyes.

"Bye," he said and she leaned towards him for one last good bye kiss. Then, she climbed out of the car, ran up the sidewalk, and turned to wave before walking through the door.

Robbie drove home in silence. He was exhausted. He fell down on his bed and was asleep before his head even hit the pillow.

September 2, 2010

Robbie awoke the next morning to a blaring rock song. He opened his eyes and looked around and saw his brother Ryan sitting by his stereo.

"Guess whose home?" Ryan laughed before turning off the radio, "Rise and shine Sleeping Beauty, we have some catching up to do."

Robbie sat up, rubbing his eyes, "How was the trip?"

"Amazing. The beach was gorgeous. See, I gotta tan," Ryan said, stretching his arms towards Robbie.

Ryan had been on a trip with his fiancée and her family. Robbie hadn't realized it was time for him to come back home.

"Aren't you supposed to be in school?"

"Yeah. They think I have mono, it's all good. Just gonna stay home a couple days. Cindy's dad gave me an early birthday present, wanna see it?"

"Sure."

"You gotta come outside. It won't fit in the house."

Robbie looked confused a moment, then stood and followed Ryan out of his room. He walked down the stairs and out the door.

Next to his truck, a copper convertible was parked.

"Cool, huh?" Ryan said proudly.

"Not as cool as my truck," Robbie said nonchalantly.

"Whatever. Wanna go for a ride later?"

"Sure. I have plans with Lydia though, so we can't stay out too late."

"Awesome. So you're still with Lydia, little bro?"

"Yeah, I don't plan on that changing any time soon."

Robbie went upstairs to take a shower and get dressed. He checked his phone. He had two texts from Alex and one from Sam. Alex was rambling about this hot girl he'd seen at his job. And Sam was wanting to hang out.

He texted Alex back, "thats awesome, go for it." and Sam "sorry, Ryan is home and I have plans with Lydia later."

Sam responded by calling him mean names and Alex didn't respond. He climbed in the shower and once he was done pulled on a black T-shirt and ripped blue jeans. Once he was downstairs, he pulled on his denim Converse.

"Ready?" Ryan asked from the kitchen, shoving a handful of popcorn into his mouth.

"Let me eat something first," Robbie replied, opening the refrigerator and grabbing a go-box from KFC.

After filling his stomach with the nutritious breakfast of fried chicken and corn, he followed Ryan out the door and climbed into the convertible. Ryan pushed a button and the roof retracted.

They took off down the road and soon they were in the country. The radio was blaring and the wind was hitting Robbie hard in the face. Now he knew why Ryan had worn sunglasses.

"So, you and Cindy are still getting married in November?" Robbie asked.

"That's the plan," Ryan yelled over the radio and wind.

"Cool... me and Lydia have been together three years in December."

"Sweet."

They rounded the corner to see a cow standing in the middle of the street.

Ryan yanked the wheel to the right to avoid hitting it and the last thing Robbie saw was the road and sky switching places before everything went black. The car flipped and rolled a couple times before stopping, resting upside down in a soybean field.

The next thing Robbie knew, he could hear people yelling and the beeping of some machine. He could feel air rushing past his body; he was on something, moving fast. He tried to open his eyes, but the light hurt them, so he closed them and fell back into a deep sleep.

September 4, 2010

Robbie opened his eyes and looked around. He realized he was in a hospital room.

"God, finally you're awake," he heard Lydia say and then he turned his head slightly to look at her. He winced when he felt a pain in his neck and head.

"Well don't move, you were just in a car wreck," she said, standing and walking over to him, "Alex and Sam were here earlier, but they had to leave."

"Oh..." he was trying to move, but everything hurt.

"You feeling okay?"

"A little achy... but yeah, pretty good," he smiled weakly at her.

She bit her lower lip, "... you don't know yet... do you?" her eyes were very sad.

"Know what?" he asked, suddenly concerned.

"Ryan... Ryan died."

"What?" Robbie said, feeling a chill run down his spine.

"When the car flipped, it was tilted so that most of the car's weight was on the driver's side and since it was a convertible, there was nothing there to protect him."

He sat there a moment, trying to take it in, "I'm sorry," she took his hand.

The door opened and his parents walked in, "Robbie, oh thank God you're okay!" his mother cried out walking to his bedside. Lydia quietly left the room, "We thought we were gonna lose you too for a moment there."

"Why?" he asked, confused.

"Your heart stopped... it wasn't beating for two whole minutes. The doctors were about to give up, but then there was a blip and it started up again. It's a miracle you're alive, the car was on top of both of you," she began to cry; Robbie assumed it was because of Ryan and the fact that she still had at least one son. Mrs. Pierce was a short, heavy-set woman with a round face outlined with wavy auburn hair. Her round blue eyes were red, most likely from crying.

She stood and walked out of the room, followed by her husband. Mr. Pierce was a tall man with short brown hair and brown eyes framed by round glasses.

After his parents left the room, Robbie felt very strange. How was he still alive? He'd even felt the car coming down on him, felt himself being crushed against the ground. He also felt as if everything was different than before he'd went out in the car with Ryan. Not just the injuries, just... everything felt weird. Maybe it was because Ryan was dead now... he would never be there again...

September 8, 2010

Robbie's dad helped him out of the wheelchair and into the car. He was still terribly sore, but the hospital had thought it'd be okay to send him home. Home. The word sounded weird knowing that Ryan wouldn't be there... ever again. He knew Cindy and her family would be coming down for the funeral. He wasn't sure he wanted to see them. He wasn't sure when the funeral would be. He wasn't sure of anything at the moment, everything he did felt strange and unfamiliar.

Once he got home, he made his way up to his room. He sat down at the computer but felt like someone was watching him. He looked up and saw a shadow by his door. He stood up and slowly walked toward the door. But when he got there, it was nothing, just a trick of the light. He shut his door and lay down on his bed.

September 13, 2010

Robbie pulled into the school parking lot. It was going to be his first day back since the accident. He looked around himself. It felt strange to be back at school. As soon as he climbed out of the car, he felt something hit his shoulder. He turned around and saw Alex and Sam attempting to hide behind Sam's Jeep. He looked down and saw a Nerf ball on the ground.

"Hey," he said, giving them a weak wave.

Once they realized they'd been discovered, they approached him, "I heard about Ryan... sorry man," Alex said, patting his shoulder. Robbie winced. Alex had brown hair in a crew cut and a small mustache and goatee. When the light hit his dark brown eyes just right, they appeared to be violet.

"Dude, don't touch him, he was in a fatal car crash!" Sam said, hitting Alex. Sam on the other hand was tall with short black hair and bangs that came down just past his eyebrows and beneath his brows were olive eyes.

"Well, sorry, it was an attempt to comfort him."

"I think all you did was hurt him."

Robbie just stared at them blankly. Strange how all their stupid bickering had been funny just a few days ago. Now it seemed juvenile and a little bit annoying.

"You okay?" Sam asked, looking up at Robbie, who had an expression on his face that was a mixture of confusion and distaste. But maybe it was just because the sun was in his eyes.

"I guess... it's weird being back at school," his voice trailed off as he looked across the parking lot. That boy... he looked familiar... Robbie felt a sudden knot in his gut when he realized the boy looked just like Ryan!

"Whoa, what the hell?" he said, under his breath, walking toward the boy. He had the same spiky blonde hair, the same lanky build, but he couldn't see his face.

Suddenly the boy turned to him. It was Ryan! But he was different. His eyes were bloodshot, making his blue irises stand out and he had deep bruises around them from where his sunglasses had been pressed into his face. He had black stains all over his face and neck and his clothes. He was wearing the same white Hollister T-shirt he'd been wearing the day of the wreck, so much blood... everything seemed to vibrate strangely almost pulse. Robbie cried out and fell backwards.

"Robbie! Robbie!" he heard a muffled voice calling his name, it seemed like it was far away, "Robbie!" someone was shaking him, *"Robbie!"* the voice was clearer now, it was Alex. Sam and Lydia were standing close by, staring at him; concerned.

"You alright?" Alex asked.

Robbie was still shook up, but he looked around for Ryan. He was gone. Maybe it'd just been his imagination.

"Yeah... yeah, I'm fine," Sam helped him to his feet and Lydia wrapped her arms around his arm.

He looked down at her for a moment, then headed for the school's entrance. His classes weren't engrossing and he often found himself staring off into space or looking around the room at random things.

When lunch came, he sat down at one of the tables that was outside. He wasn't really hungry but he figured he should eat. He picked up his sandwich and looked up. And saw Ryan standing by the cafeteria entrance.

He merely stared at Robbie, the same piercing, angry look in his eyes. The rest of his face was blank, emotionless. He looked to the right and then someone passed in front of him and when they were gone, so was Ryan.

"Robbie," Lydia's voice broke through the soundless, pulsing barrier that had surrounded Robbie.

"Hey," he said quietly, setting down his sandwich. He stood and tossed his plate into the nearest trashcan.

"Why aren't you eating lunch?"

"Not hungry," he replied, shrugging.

She just looked at him and shook her head.

Robbie was apprehensive the rest of the day, scared that he would see Ryan again. When he got home, he turned on his computer and typed in a new social site status: "don't people who are dying start seeing dead people towards the end? what about those who almost died, but recovered? does that happen to them too?"

September 16, 2010

Lydia helped Robbie straighten his tie and then backed up to look at him, "You're gorgeous you know."

He just looked straight ahead, a solemn expression on his face with a hint of sadness.

"You never smile anymore."

"Not happy about anything."

She sighed, "Well, I guess we should go inside," she climbed out of the truck and looked back. He hadn't moved to follow her, "Robbie, come on."

He slowly turned and opened the door. She came around to his side of the car and grabbed his hand, leading him into the church.

Right before they entered the church, he turned to her, "I really don't want to go in there with all those people... I really just want to be left alone."

"Robbie... you need to go. He was your brother."

"Yeah... I know," he said, turning and walking through the door.

He shook many people's hands and nodded to condolences with the same blank expression on his face; he didn't really listen to what they said. He rarely said a word, but held Lydia's hand through it all.

He was looking for the pew his parents were sitting in when Cindy walked up to him.

"Oh, Robbie," she said, hugging him tightly. He hugged back with his free arm, but his expression remained the same solemn one he'd been wearing all day, "I still can't believe he's gone," she let go and wiped her eyes. "It was just a couple more months 'til we were supposed to get married."

"Yeah, I know."

He walked away from her; he really wasn't in the mood to talk about Ryan. He found his parents seated near the front, sharing a pew with Cindy's parents. He sat down next to his mother and Lydia sat on his other side. The visitation service started not too long after that. Robbie could feel Lydia holding his hand and resting her head on his shoulder and he could hear his mother crying next to him. But none of that seemed so real as Ryan, standing in the doorway that led to the baptistery. He stood there through the whole service, staring at Robbie. And Robbie stared back.

Once the visitation was over, Robbie led Lydia out of the church and to his truck; he wanted to avoid having to be around people who were all going to say the same thing. It was all boring and frankly, he didn't want to talk about Ryan. They both sat in the truck for a while, an awkward silence between them. It was a new experience; they'd never had those awkward silences before.

"So... you want me to take you home now?"

"I guess, if you're ready to leave," Lydia was a little worried, he'd had the same expression on his face and same tone of voice for a week now. It had changed a bit, there was occasionally a twitch or different pitch, but it was very small and seldom.

"Okay... hey," he looked up at her, "Sorry our plans on the second got ruined."

"It wasn't your fault... I'm more upset about Ryan dying."

"Okay," he started the truck and drove her home. When he got to her house, she leaned over and kissed him. He looked at her without turning his head.

"Well, bye. See you later. I love you."

"Love you too," he replied quietly as she climbed out of the truck.

September 18, 2010

Robbie's mom walked into his room quietly. He was sitting at his computer, playing Spider Solitaire. He'd been doing that nearly every time she came in his room since the accident.

"Robbie," he looked up at her. He had dark purple bags under his eyes, "Have you not been sleeping well?"

He stared at her for a moment, "I've slept some."

"Maybe you should do something other than sit around all day staring at that computer. Like, go out with Alex and Sam or go over to Lydia's."

"I don't want to."

"Robbie, Ryan is dead. He has been for two weeks now. You're the only son I have left... please, be my son."

"I know he's dead... I was there when it happened. Now please leave and let me play my game."

"Robbie-"

"Please."

His mother stood there a moment longer then left. She returned a few moments later, "It'd also be nice if you'd eat."

"Okay," she stood there, as if waiting for something, "Mom."

"Yes."

"I... see Ryan... sometimes."

He saw her tense up, "What?"

"Never mind."

"No, what did you say?"

"It was dumb."

"You've seen Ryan... since the accident?"

"Yes."

"... do you wanna talk about it?"

"Not really."

"Why not? You brought it up."

"It was a mistake," he turned off the computer and went to lay on his bed.

She slowly left the room.

Instant Messenger (5:30 A.M.)

Mariah Pierce: does Robbie talk to you about the accident?
Lydia Farmer: not rlly, he just says things feel weird sometimes
Mariah Pierce: he told me something the other night that disturbed me...
Lydia Farmer: ?
Mariah Pierce: he said he's seen Ryan... since the accident
Lydia Farmer: what!??
Mariah Pierce: yes, he didn't want to talk about it after he brought it up
Lydia Farmer: hm... he nvr rlly wants 2 talk about ANYTHING anymore..
Mariah Pierce: so it isn't just at home?
Lydia Farmer: no, he does it @ school 2
Mariah Pierce: I'm really worried about him
Lydia Farmer: me2
Mariah Pierce: will you try to talk to him... if he'll open up to anyone, it's you
Lydia Farmer: I'll try, cant promise anything with him the way hes been
Mariah Pierce: thank you, dear, it means a lot

Lydia Farmer: I kno... I love him
Mariah Pierce: I know you do, sweetie,
and he loves you too... he's just had an
odd way of showing it lately
Mariah Pierce: well, I'm getting off, time
to wake up Robbie
Lydia Farmer: ttyl mrs pierce
Mariah Pierce is offline.

The school day itself went by quick
and uneventful. After school, Lydia
approached Robbie, "Hey, my parents needed
my car today, the van has been giving them
fits, think you could take me home?"

"Yeah," he said dryly, avoiding eye
contact.

"Thanks," the contrast of her chipper
tone and his nonchalant one could have been
comical under different circumstances.

They were silent most of the ride to
her house. When Robbie parked next to the
curb, she saw her chance, "Robbie, are you
okay?"

"I suppose."

"I mean, you've seemed different
since the accident... is something bothering
you?" she bit her lower lip.

"Well, there is the fact Ryan died.
And-" his voice caught in his throat, "oh, you
wouldn't believe me anyway."

"What?" he was silent, staring straight ahead, "Robbie, I care about you, God, I'm in love with you. What's wrong?"

He winced, showing the most emotion Lydia had seen in him since the accident, "I... I see Ryan sometimes. But he's... different, just like everything else. He looks like he would have right after the accident, he's all bruised and bloody... and he just stares at me. He never says a word; he never does anything but stare," he looked over at Lydia, "You think I'm crazy don't you?"

"No," she said, not sure if she believed the words coming out of her mouth, "I just think you're... emotionally worked up. That accident and Ryan's death... they were both very traumatic experiences. I think you just need time."

"I think my mom wants me to see a shrink."

There was a long silence, "... do you want to come in? Mom and Dad won't be back 'til seven, at the earliest."

"I suppose," he replied quietly. They walked into her house and she got a Coke out of the fridge. Robbie didn't want any; it was the first time Lydia had ever seen him turn down a Coke. She grabbed his hand and led him up the stairs to her room. He stood in the doorway as she made her way to the bed. She sat the soda on her nightstand, then lay on her side, looking at Robbie.

He looked back at her for a moment, then slowly walked into the room. He looked like an animal in an unfamiliar place. He lay down beside her, putting his arm around her waist, holding her close. They both lay there a moment, still. Then Robbie moved his head around Lydia's shoulder and kissed her throat gently. Then he moved up to her jaw, kissing her again. She could feel his breath on her neck as he rested his cheek against where her shoulder met her neck.

She felt stimulated and yet at the same time she was frightened, frightened that he would suddenly do something unexpected, something... bad. She didn't know why she felt this way, this was the most action she'd gotten out of him in a while

He lifted his head and kissed her throat again. There was a moment of awkward silence, "Lydia," he broke the silence, his voice the same flat tone it'd been for weeks, "I love you with all my heart and soul... I'm just not sure where either of them has gone," she swallowed, "You're scared of me... aren't you?"

"No," she said quietly, "I'm just... scared for you. I'm worried about you. Ever since the accident, you haven't been... the same."

"Nothing has been the same."

She lay there in silence and he kissed her one more time before laying his head on the pillow and pulling her closer to him, "I feel lost... and alone. Like I'm sleepwalking. Everything is foreign. You could almost say I'm afraid, but I don't feel afraid. I only have one fear... and that is losing you."

She felt a chill run down her spine. She couldn't decide if she wanted to snuggle closer or pull away from him. She decided to remain where she was. She felt her eyelids grow heavy and as hard as she fought it, unconsciousness came over her. When she awoke, Robbie was gone.

<u>September 22, 2010</u>

Robbie made his way through the cemetery. He was in some of the nicest clothes he owned; a white button up shirt, a charcoal jacket and pants, some shiny black Dockers, and a blue and black striped tie. He was completely alone; apparently no one else had decided to visit graves today.

He stopped at a particularly polished granite headstone. It read:

Ryan Alexander Pierce.
December 14, 1990 - September 2, 2010

He looked at the small bouquet of delphinium belladonna in his hand. He frowned and looked out over the rest of the cemetery. Then he looked back down at the headstone.

"I know we're guys and we don't really get into flowers and all that jazz, but I thought it was only right to bring some..." he bent down and laid the delphinium belladonna on the rim that jutted out around the base of the stone, "You know, I see you almost every day, but it's not the same as it used to be... nothing is the same as it used to be... and I miss you."

And for the first time since the accident, he cried. The salt in his tears burned his eyes and the burn made him realize he couldn't remember the last time he'd cried.

He laid down on his back on a plot of unused ground next to Ryan's tombstone, resting his head on his hands, "Why is it that this is the place I feel most at home?..." he glanced over at Ryan's tombstone, then down at the ground, "Can you hear me down there?"

Suddenly, Ryan appeared, standing over him, his eyes piercing.

"Holy shit!" Robbie cried out, flailing and sitting up suddenly. But Ryan wasn't there.

"Why do you do this?" he began to cry again as he stood and wiped the dirt and grass shavings from his clothes, "Are you mad because I lived? Well, I didn't choose to live. I didn't choose for you to die. There are times that I feel *dead* inside."

He stood, waiting for a response from Ryan, and when he got none, he tromped out of the graveyard and headed home.

When he got home, he could hear his parents yelling inside.

"Mariah, it's not a good idea!"

"Well, it's too late, I already called her."

"Why didn't you ask me first?"

"Because every time we've talked about it, you get like this!" her voice softened, "He needs help, John."

"What's going on?" Robbie asked, coming through the door.

They both stood there a moment, looking like children caught with their hands in the cookie jar.

Robbie's father cleared his throat, "Your mother thinks you need to see a shr-" he decided to change words, "*counselor*, to help you sort out everything that's happened."

"Everything that's happened?..."

"The accident sweetie and..." her voice trailed off and her husband finished for her, "Ryan's death."

"I don't really want to talk about that," Robbie started up the stairs.

24

"But you need to talk things through."

"Whatever you say," he headed up the stairs without giving them a chance to respond.

September 25, 2010

"Hello Robbie, I am Doctor Belinda Wilder. I talk with people who need to get things off their chest or solve subconscious problems. I also help those who have been through traumatic experiences," she raised one eyebrow. She had overly dyed blonde hair and wrinkles it appeared she was trying to hide with aloe lotion or something like that, "So, let's begin with the accident. How much do you remember?"

He sat there a moment, staring out the window.

"Robbie, I need you to talk to me... your parents are paying good money for my time, let's not waste it, shall we."

"I don't remember much... there was a cow in the road and Ryan yanked the wheel... and we flipped... then I woke up in the hospital."

"And Ryan?"

Robbie sat in a long silence that seemed to drag on for hours, "............... he died."

"So Ryan is dead, yes?"

"Yes."

"Then how have you seen him? Your parents mentioned you saying you'd seen him since the accident."

"I don't know... I just do."

"Do what?"

"You won't believe me."

"Try me."

"No."

"Robbie."

"......"

"I only want to help."

"I don't want or need any help."

"Your parents don't see it that way."

"I know they don't."

"Please tell me what you 'just do'."

"........ I see Ryan... he's standing there, looking at me, but he's....... dead."

"Like a ghost?"

"I guess."

"How often do you see him?"

"I don't know, I don't really keep track."

"Do you think about him often?"

"Often enough."

"Do you ever cry about him?"

"No."

"Does it make you feel bad that you don't cry?"

"I don't know... hadn't given it much thought."

"What do you, I mean, what have you felt since the accident?"

"Like I'm alone."

"Alone? How?"

"I don't know how to explain it... it's almost like I'm in a dream, like everyone is miles away from me."

"Do you have a special someone?"

"A girlfriend? Yeah."

"What's her name?"

"Lydia."

"Do you feel like she's miles away from you?"

"...... not as many miles as everyone else, but she's still not as close as I'd like her to be."

"Have you pushed her away?"

"I don't know, maybe."

"That's the end of our time, Robbie. I'll see you in about a week."

"Uh-huh," Robbie stood and walked out of the office.

His parents were out in the waiting room and Doctor Wilder beckoned them into her office. Robbie sat down in a chair near the reception desk. His parents came out after about five minutes and they all got in the car to head home.

There was no talking until they turned onto their street, "So, what's she think is wrong with me?" Robbie asked.

"She thinks you have survivor's guilt," his mother replied.

"Oh, okay."

September 26, 2010

Robbie looked around. He was in the hospital again. His gaze stopped at the door. A young woman, college age Robbie guessed, was leaning against the doorframe. She had dark brown shoulder length hair and mesmerizing green eyes. She was dressed in all black and had her arms crossed.

"You're awake," she said, standing up straight and uncrossing he arms.

Robbie just stared at her.

"That was some accident."

He continued to gawk at her, taken and confused. She was oddly familiar.

"Okay, so I know what you've been asking yourself," she sat down in the chair next to his bed, "How did I survive when Ryan didn't?" he tensed up when she mentioned his brother's name; how did she know his name? "You felt the car on top of you too, if it killed him, why not you too? Despite what you may think or believe, you're here for a reason."

He sat in silence a moment, then looked at her, "Nothing feels the same... why *am* I still here? I mean, I *should* have died."

"You'll find out soon enough."

He frowned, still trying to place her, "Who... who are you?"

She stood and walked over to the bed. She bent down and whispered in his ear, "You will find the answers in time. You know me, Robbie Pierce, and I know you."

As he felt a chill run down his spine, he looked around and he was in his dark room. It had been a dream... one very strange, twisted dream. But who was the girl? He knew he'd seen her before... or at least, he could've sworn she was too familiar for him not to have seen her. He looked at a clock. It was three in the morning. He decided he should try to go back to sleep.

He woke up again around six and decided to get out of bed. He walked downstairs and saw his dad sitting on the sofa, the light of the television dancing across his face. He tried to walk by, unnoticed.

"Where are you going, Robbie?"

"For a walk."

His father looked up at him in his T-shirt and jeans, "In that? Your mother would throw a fit, put on a jacket."

He turned and headed back upstairs without the typical teenage breath blowing and eye roll. He grabbed his leather jacket and pulled it on. As he did, he caught a glimpse of himself in the mirror. He paused and stopped to look at himself. His skin was so pale it looked almost white against the contrast of his black jacket and dark brown hair. The bags around his eyes made his eyes dark and unwelcoming. The rest of his face was in a frown, but there didn't seem to be much feeling behind it.

He turned away from the mirror and walked out the door. He didn't know where he was going, he just wanted to walk. So he did. He walked for what seemed like hours and mere seconds at the same time. He didn't really pay attention to where he was going; for that matter, he didn't pay attention to much of anything and miraculously no cars hit him. Everything was really blurred and unclear until he stopped in front of Lydia's house.

He didn't know why he stopped or why he'd bothered to look at this house when he'd ignored all the rest. He checked his phone for the time; it was about 7:14 A.M.

He wasn't sure if Lydia would be awake, but he didn't care. He walked up to the door and knocked. He waited a moment. A moment longer... he raised his fist to knock again when the door opened and he was eye to eye with Lydia's father, still shirtless and in pajama pants.

"Robbie?" he squinted as the first beams of sunlight hit him in the face. He was a stout man with a gruff face and gray hair, though the top of his head was completely bald, "What are you doing here at this hour?"

"I couldn't sleep, so I went for a walk... ended up here and thought I'd see if Lydia was awake."

"Went for a walk? Son, you walked one hell of a ways all because of insomnia."

It was true; Lydia's house was about five miles from Robbie's.

"Yeah... I guess. Is she up?"

"I dunno. I suppose I could check," Robbie stepped toward the door, "*You* stay here," Mr. Farmer glared at him then disappeared inside.

Robbie had known for a while that Lydia's father wasn't his biggest fan. For one, he thought he and Lydia were too involved. For another, they'd been steady for almost three years, he wasn't a school girl's crush that was going to disappear in a few months. He supposed it was understandable; Lydia was the only child the Farmers had and it would be natural to dislike the thing that's going to take her away from them sooner or later.

A movement behind the door snapped Robbie out of his reverie. Instead of Mr. Farmer's scowling face he was greeted by Lydia's smile.

"Hey," she said, "You're up early."

"Yeah, couldn't sleep," his mind went back to his dream.

"Did you really walk all the way out here?"

"Yeah."

Her expression turned serious, "Is something wrong?" so did her tone.

"Not really... just went for a walk."

"And ended up at my house?"

"Yes."

There was another one of those awkward silences they hadn't had before.

"You wanna walk with me?" he asked quietly.

"Sure," she smiled and grabbed his hand. They walked a little ways down to the park, then sat down on the swings.

Lydia was looking out over the sunrise when Robbie's voice broke her out of her hypnotism, "My parents made me see a counselor."

"Oh?"

"Yeah, they seem to think I have some problem because of the accident or Ryan's death or both."

"And what'd the counselor say?"

"She thinks I have survivor's guilt."

"Well, maybe-"

"I died... in the hospital," he said it so quietly, looking at the ground and not seeming to talk to anyone.

"What? No, Robbie, what are you talking about?"

"My heart stopped. My heart sat still for two minutes. For two minutes I was dead."

"But that doesn't mean you were dead."

"Lydia, when your heart stops, you're dead... how could I have survivor's guilt when I didn't survive?"

"But, you're alive. You're here, right now... with me."

"Yeah... I don't know," he looked at her and she saw a look in his eyes she'd never seen before, "I guess it's just... never mind."

"What?"

"Never mind."

She crossed her arms over her chest.

"Sorry, I just don't know what to say," he said, looking back at the ground.

A breeze picked up and Lydia shivered, rubbing her arms.

"You cold?" he asked, looking at her thin sweater.

"Yeah, I thought it was warmer out."

"Here," he took off his jacket and handed it to her.

"But aren't you cold?" she asked, looking at his bare white arms.

"No, I don't really get cold. I only wore it so Mom wouldn't throw a fit."

Lydia reluctantly took the jacket, putting her arms through the large sleeves and wrapping the front around herself. The jacket smelled like him and the scent sent a pleasant chill down her spine.

Even in his jacket, he could see her cheeks and nose turning red, "We should get you back home, I don't want you getting sick on account of me," he stood and stretched his arms.

"No, we can stay, I'm fine."

"Come on. If you get sick out here, your dad'll kil-" he stopped short, "-be very displeased with me."

She slowly stood and he put his arm around her shoulders to help keep her warm. When they got back to her house, she handed him his jacket.

"You can come in for a while, you know."

He looked up at the door and saw Mr. Farmer's shadow looming there, "I don't think that's the best idea. I'll see you later."

He stood there and she leaned into him, then he looked down and kissed her on the lips for the first time since the accident. She ran up the stairs and into the house; he almost swore he could hear Mr. Farmer bellowing about staying out too long in the brisk weather.

He walked most of the way home carrying his jacket, but when he rounded the corner onto his street, he put it back on to keep up a show for his mom.

September 30, 2010

"You're going to be eighteen in a little over a week," Robbie's mom said, coming into his room.

"Yeah."

"Aren't you excited?"

"I guess, it's just a number."

"But it's a *big* number. Soon you'll be able to vote and buy tobacco products... but please promise me you won't buy any tobacco products."

"I won't. I've never wanted to smoke anyway."

"So who all are you inviting over?" It was a Pierce family tradition to have some friends and family over on the family member's actual birthday.

"I dunno, probably Lydia, Sam, and Alex."

"That's all?"

"Yeah."

She shrugged, "Alright," she stood in the doorway a moment, looked as if she'd suddenly remembered something, and darted out of the room.

October

"So Robbie, how are you feeling today?" Dr. Wilder asked, glancing at the clipboard on her crossed legs.

"Fine, I guess."

"That's good. Anything interesting going on? Maybe at school?"

"My eighteenth birthday is coming up."

"Oh, that's exciting!"

"Yeah, I guess."

"What do you mean I g-"

"Dr. Wilder, if your heart stops, are you dead?"

"Well, I don't know Robbie. I suppose it would seem that way, but you can restart the heart with the technology we have these days, but you can't bring someone back from the dead."

"But you're just laying there and everything stops, there's no signs of life. You're not really different than a corpse in that regard."

"But you can revive someone who's heart's stopped; you can't revive a corpse.

Robbie, where are these questions coming from?"

"... just something I read, that I was wondering about."

"I see, a controversy on when someone is truly is dead? Why would you be reading such material?"

"It wasn't because it was about death, it was because I know someone who's had their heart restarted and I was curious about the subject."

"You think they could have 'restarted' Ryan?"

"He has nothing to do with this... I have to use the restroom, please excuse me," he stood up, frowning, and walked to the restroom.

<u>October 8, 2010</u>

"Happy birthday to you! Happy birthday to you! Happy birthday dear Robbie! Happy birthday to you!" his family and Lydia sang out; Sam and Alex weren't there.

"Make a wish, sweetie," his mom said quietly compared to the song.

He sat there a moment and then leaned in and blew out all his candles. Everyone clapped and his mom began to cut the cake.

"My Robbie is eighteen," Lydia said, smiling and wrapping her arms around his neck. He just looked back at her, "You could smile more."

He forced a small smile, but she thought his eyes seemed happy for a second or two.

"Doctors say it's healthy to smile and laugh, you might get some of your color back if you did more of those," she kissed his cheek.

Mrs. Pierce was heading to the kitchen to clean off the serving knife and candles when her sister, Elaine Moscow, grabbed her arm, "What's wrong with Robbie?"

Mrs. Pierce took a deep breath, "He's been that way since the accident... Ryan's death really took its toll on him," she bit her lower lip and fought back tears at the mention of her older son.

"I understand, but, wow. He looks awful Mariah."

"I know. He won't sleep. He won't eat. He's just not himself."

"There there," Ms. Moscow put her arm around her sister, "Have you tried to help him?"

"Yes, but he won't talk to me and John. We've had him going to a counselor.

He was supposed to go today, but we called it off since it was his birthday."

"Is she helping?"

"I don't know, she seems to think he has survivor's guilt."

"That would make sense... let's stop talking about this, it's supposed to be a happy day, Robbie is eighteen today."

A knock came at the door and Robbie answered it. It was Sam.

"Hey, sorry I'm late," he said, blushing a little, "Alex couldn't come, he had stuff to do."

"He doesn't wanna be here," Robbie said quietly. Things hadn't been the greatest between Robbie, Sam, and Alex. His mono-tone ways had been driving Alex crazy and slowly Alex had started to think Robbie *was* crazy. They'd stopped talking when Alex had exploded on Robbie about being a sad sack and lying about seeing dead people for attention in the library. Sam had tried playing it neutral. He wanted to be friends with both Robbie and Alex.

"Okay," Sam sighed and stepped in the door, "Here's your present. Sorry, I fail at wrapping presents." It was a football. "I noticed your old one getting kind of tattered the last time we played. Wanna go test it out?"

"Sure," Robbie said quietly, heading out the door. He, Lydia, and Sam made their way around the house to the backyard and Sam ran out to the fence; Robbie stood up by the house and Lydia sat down on the bench swing to watch.

Before throwing the ball, Robbie rubbed his right shoulder. He could feel the line where they'd had to stitch him up. They'd told him it was a bad wound, but he'd never really noticed much pain. He drew back his arm and threw. It didn't hurt, at all.

Sam caught it perfectly and threw it back to Robbie, who caught it. They threw it back and forth for a while, no one speaking; they didn't have anything to say.

"So, nice ball?" Sam asked, after landing from a jump catch.

"Yeah, I guess. Kind of boring."

"What!? You used to love football." Sam looked completely astonished; so did Lydia.

"Times change."

"Yeah..." Sam looked at the ball in his hands, then walked to Robbie, "I guess we'll stop playing for now," he handed Robbie the ball.

Once they were inside, Sam pulled Lydia to the side, "He doesn't like football anymore. What else is different?"

"He's different, haven't you noticed."

"Well, at least he talks to you. He hasn't talked to me or Alex in forever. I know he doesn't eat lunch anymore."

"Yeah... he doesn't eat much anymore."

"Is he depressed or something... about Ryan?"

"I guess that's part of it. The counselor he's been seeing thinks he has survivor's guilt."

"He's been seeing a counselor?" Sam sounded surprised.

"His mom's idea."

"Well, I think I'm gonna hit the road, I think things'll just get awkward if I stay. Bye," he hugged her, then said bye to Robbie and left.

His aunt and his dad's parents left not too long after Sam and then his cousin, Allison, who was Ryan's age, left. Once it started to get dark outside, Lydia decided it was time for her to head home.

"Happy birthday, Robbie," she said, kissing his forehead and leaving.

"She's a nice girl, Robbie," Mr. Pierce said once she'd gone out the door.

"Yeah," Robbie smiled slightly.

Robbie was heading to his truck, he had seen Ryan more that day than any other day. He just wanted to get home. He looked up and Ryan was standing by his truck. And for the first time since Robbie had started seeing him, Ryan did something. He motioned to Robbie; it was a hand gesture that hinted he wanted Robbie to follow him. He felt a chill run down his spine, he was scared of what he would find if he followed Ryan but he also felt as if he had no choice but to follow him.

He looked across the parking lot and saw Lydia. He practically ran across the parking lot to her, "Lydia, will you come home with me?"

She looked at him like he was crazy, but saw true anxiety in his eyes, the most emotion she'd seen in him in a while, "Sure."

She climbed in the truck and they started down the road. Ryan kept appearing at the side of the road, like a jumping trail marker. It didn't take long for Lydia to realize they weren't headed to Robbie's house.

"Where are we going?"

"I don't know," he kept his eyes on the road.

"How can you not know!?"

"Because I'm following Ryan... he wants me to go somewhere, I don't know where and I'm scared. I wouldn't wanna go alone or with anyone else but you," he glanced at her, then back at the road.

Ryan stood in the entry way to a cave and then he was gone. Robbie pulled over and climbed out of the truck. He walked into the cave. Lydia reluctantly followed.

Robbie heard a sound, it sounded like a scream, but it was silent, as if they were struggling to make the sound. There was also a sound like scuffling on the cave floor. He walked toward the sound and he saw a dark shadow, but he couldn't make it out.

"Do you hear that?" he asked Lydia.

"Hear what?" she seemed completely oblivious.

He walked closer to the sound and shadow. It seemed to move away from him as he approached it, as if it were his own shadow. He was able to make what looked like a man's head and shoulders and he was struggling with something on the ground...

"Do you see that?" Robbie asked incredulously.

"No," Lydia responded

"How can you not see it, it's right there."

"I don't see anything... Robbie, come on, let's go."

"Does it really bother you that much?"

"What, the fact that you keep seeing your dead brother? The fact that you're a freak? Yes, it does."

"What'd you say?" he turned to her, an anger burning in his eyes.

"Nothing."

"No, what did you call me?"

She stood there, silent.

"Did you just call me a freak?"

She swallowed, "Yes."

His eyes were piercing slits as he approached her, "I'm a freak?"

"Robbie, stop it, you're scaring me."

"I'm scaring you? It's because you don't understand me, that's how people are, things they don't understand scare them. Did any of you stop to think that this is scaring me too? And that all of you acting scared of me isn't helping?" He was slowly drawing nearer to her.

"You're not gonna hurt me, are you Robbie?"

"You think I'm gonna hurt you?" he paused for a moment. Then suddenly, he grabbed her by her shoulders, pushing her against the wet cave wall. She heard him fumbling around in his pocket. Then he pulled his hand out and she was terrified he had a knife or something like that.

"Oh, no, Robbie, please don't! Please, oh God, Robbie, please don't!" she was screaming and frantically pushing him away. She could feel him moving his arm up. His other arm did not slacken, his elbow was locked, keeping her pressed against the wall.

"Robbie, please, don't! No! No! No! Robbie, please!" she looked into his piercing eyes, she was crying now, screaming, hitting him. She saw something glint in the small amount of light in the cave, "Robbie! Please no!"

He released her and she almost fell to the ground. She was breathing hard and quickly began wiping the tears from her eyes. She looked up at Robbie. His back was turned to her. His arm hung by his side, his cell phone in his hand.

"You really thought I was gonna hurt you..." he said quietly.

She was silent.

"You know I wouldn't do that."

"Robbie, I don't even feel like I know you anymore."

He was silent for a moment, "Come on, Lydia, I'll take you home..." he headed for the entrance of the cave, leaving her alone.

She followed him shortly and they were silent the whole ride to her house. He frowned straight ahead and she stared absently out the window.

When they pulled up to the curb in front of Lydia's house, Robbie took a deep breath, "Lydia, I would never hurt you."

She sat for a moment, tears welling up in her eyes, then she sniffed and regained her composure. Her voice wavered, "You've already hurt me more than anyone ever has."

She opened the door and climbed out of the truck. When she turned back to shut the door, she saw him staring at where she'd just been sitting, a look of mixed dismay and deep remorse on his otherwise blank face.

"Bye," she said quietly. He made no response and she shut the door and walked up to her house. Once she was inside, he pulled away from the curb.

<u>October 14, 2010</u>

Robbie finished brushing his teeth and then looked at himself closely in the mirror. He leaned in and rubbed his chin. He was as clean shaven as a baby. There was no stubble whatsoever. Suddenly it struck him as odd since he couldn't remember the last time he'd shaved. He stared in the mirror a moment longer, then scratched his head and went into his room.

He turned on his computer. He opened the web browser and the news section of his homepage filled the screen. And that was when he saw her.

Her picture was next to the headline 'Still No Suspect in Bivens' Murder'; she was the girl from his dream. He clicked the headline to read the article. Marcy Bivens, age nineteen, was found strangled to death in one of the caves out in the local woods. It is also thought that some sexual activity took place, due to a condom wrapper found at the scene. But currently, the police still have no leads. Police chief Albert Straum had this to say, "He's one smart guy, he raped her with a condom so he couldn't be matched by tests run on her then killed her so she'd keep her mouth shut."

He couldn't believe it. Next to this story were stories that went back, past updates on the Bivens murder/rape case. He clicked the oldest headline: Teen Found Dead in Local Caves. The date was September 2, 2010. But that couldn't be. *That* was crazy... that was the same day Ryan had been killed in their freak car accident.

"All because of a stupid cow," Robbie thought, frowning in frustration. His brother

48

had died because of a cow... he knew it was terrible but he found himself hoping it'd already found its way to the butcher shop and suffered a slow butchering like they show in those vegetarian videos.

He lay down on his bed and stared angrily at the ceiling. He'd felt anger a lot lately; anger towards his mom, anger towards Lydia, anger towards Alex... he hadn't felt much of anything since the accident until recently and then it only seemed that he felt mad or sad.

His frown began to melt when he thought of Lydia. She'd told him he'd hurt her... more than anyone had. He would never hurt her intentionally; he had never wanted to hurt her. He had called her and she hadn't picked up. She hadn't replied when he'd texted her. He assumed she was still upset with him.

<u>October 15, 2010</u>

After school, Robbie waited outside the doors for Lydia. When she came out, he walked over to her, "Lydia, I'm sorry about the other day. I blew up on you and I shouldn't have."

"Robbie, please leave me alone," she kept looking ahead, walking fast.

"Lydia, please."

She stopped and turned to him, but wouldn't look up at his face, "Robbie, things have not been great between us. I mean, I don't know if you've noticed it, but things just... aren't what they used to be. And I... I just need some time to think things over," she walked off, her head down. Robbie just stared after her until she was out of sight, then climbed into his truck. He had an appointment with Dr. Wilder.

"So, Robbie, how have you been?"

"Not so great... I think my girlfriend broke up with me, but I'm not sure... I don't feel capable of understanding her anymore than she is of understanding me."

"Then could this break up be a good thing?"

"I... she is the only person I come close to feeling like I did before the accident with. And... I love her."

"Isn't love a strong word for an eighteen year old to use?"

He was silent and looked up at the clock.

"No, Robbie, it's not time to leave yet."

"Doctor, I... I don't think I have survivor's guilt."

"Oh?" Dr. Wilder looked doubtful, "And why do you say this?"

"I saw another dead person."

"Who?"

"Marcy Bivens. She was murdered and I've never met her before. I didn't even know she existed until I saw her...." his voice trailed off.

"Saw her?"

"Her ghost. I guess that's what you'd call it."

"And you know you never saw her before the accident?"

"Yes."

She wrote something on her clipboard.

"I'm not crazy, doc," he said, standing up, "And no offense, but talking to you hasn't done anything to help me... not that I think I need help. I'm going to talk to my parents and more than likely you'll never see me again. Good-bye, Dr. Wilder," and he walked right out of her office, out of the building, and into his truck.

"You did what!?" were the first words out of his mother's mouth when he got home. He guessed Dr. Wilder had called her.

"She wasn't changing anything. I was still seeing Ryan and still wasn't happy."

The angry look on his mother's face softened, "You aren't happy?"

"Not really. I'm just kind of... here," he walked up the stairs and into his room. He shut the door behind him.

October 17, 2010

For the first time since early September, Robbie logged into his social profile. The first thing he saw was his profile picture. It was him and Lydia, smiling. He noticed he had what seemed like a freakish amount of color in his cheeks. He hadn't smiled like that in a long time. The next thing he noticed was that he only had one new notification. He clicked it. It read 'Lydia Farmer cancelled your relationship.'

He felt like he'd just been punched in the gut. Or lower. He clicked her name and looked at her information. Her relationship status said 'It's Complicated'. He went to his profile and changed his to the same thing, but then hid it. He looked at his picture again. He didn't look like that anymore. That wasn't who he was anymore. He shrugged; he supposed he should change it. It felt wrong to leave it as it was. He clicked 'Take New Picture With Webcam.' He looked at his webcam and clicked the button. It snapped and he looked at his new picture. It was pretty shadowy, but he could make out his pale face, dark eyes, and dark hair. He wasn't smiling. He saved it and logged out. People's lives through online updates just weren't interesting anymore.

October 20, 2010

Robbie found himself in a room that was all white. He was standing in a line and soon he realized he was at a funeral and he was in line to pass by the coffin. He assumed it was just a memory, Ryan's funeral, he saw a lot of people he knew: his parents, Sam, Alex, the Farmers, Ms. Moscow...

When it came to be his turn at the coffin he looked in, expecting to see Ryan's face caked with make up to hide the bruises. But he felt a knot form in his stomach when he saw Lydia's face; not Ryan's.

"Hey," he asked, "What happened?"

He heard his mother, "He would've been devastated."

"Mom, what's going on? What happened?" he tried to tap her shoulder but she ignored him.

"Man, that's three people in just the past few months," Alex said to Sam; Sam was crying.

"Guys, what happened to her!?" they didn't respond to him, "Hey!" he punched Sam's shoulder. He didn't even flinch.

"What the hell is going on? Can anyone hear me?"

A high pitched sound like metal scraping metal rang through the air. Robbie grabbed his ears and fell to his knees; nobody else seemed to hear it.

He looked up and saw Marcy standing over him, "What're you doing here?" he asked, his eyes welling up, "You're dead."

"I'm in your head, Robbie. The only place I can reach you is in your head," he frowned up at her, confused, "Why do you think Ryan can't talk to you?"

"Why her!? Why!?" he could see Mr. Farmer sitting in a folding chair, bawling into his hands, his wife attempting to comfort him, "I'll kill the bastard with my own two hands if I ever I find him... I'll kill him!"

"What happened?" he asked Marcy, the tears beginning to fall.

"Lydia Farmer died," she said quietly looking at her body, almost like she was in her own world, "But she isn't dead yet, Robbie," she seemed to come back to reality, "Not yet."

He saw Ryan by her coffin, nodding slowly, "Not yet," her voice was a whisper as

54

he found himself back in his room. He was in a cold sweat. He sat up and wrapped his arms around his knees and started crying. He didn't know why, he knew Lydia wasn't really dead.

But Marcy's words echoed in his head, *"Not yet..."*

He climbed out of bed and looked out the window. The first rays of sunlight were shining over the tops of houses and trees. He walked outside. He knew his mother would be throwing a fit if she saw him outside barefoot and shirtless, nothing on but his pajama pants. He walked off down the street and kept going for what he knew must be several miles because he ended up at the cemetery. He kept going too until he came to a gravestone that was decorated with flower wreaths and a stone angel.

He fell to his knees and read the inscription upon it:

Marcy Bivens
"only the good die young"
March 12, 1991 - September 2,
2010

And suddenly he felt a deep remorse inside himself, as if perhaps he'd been close to her; as if he'd lost a close friend. And he began to cry again, in heaving sobs. But they weren't sad tears, they were angry tears.

"Why!?" he yelled, anger burning in his eyes as he pulled his arm back and punched Marcy's gravestone with all his strength. He felt his knuckles split and the blood running down his hand, but he didn't care, it didn't really hurt, not nearly as bad as the mass of negative emotions inside him.

"Why why why!?" he cried angrily, pounding the stone as one would hit someone trying to comfort them while they're in a rage.

He fell to his hands and knees, the tear flow from his eyes falling to the ground like rain. He wiped his eyes with his arm, but the rain kept falling.

He looked up at the stone, breathing hard. Everything seemed to slow down. Time stood still. The only thing that stood out to him was the death date on her tombstone: September 2, 2010. It was on that day his brother had died. It was on that day that his heart had stopped; *he* had been dead for two cold minutes.

He heard footsteps behind him, but he paid them no mind. He could hear the distant wail of sirens, maybe they were right beside him and maybe they were miles away, it made no difference.

"Robbie!" he felt hands on his shoulders, the voice was so far away, yet close, "Robbie!" he slowly turned his head and found himself looking into the eyes of his mother, "Robbie!... Robbie!" she shook him slightly. He realized he felt water drops hitting his back; it was raining, not just from his eyes but from the skies as well. It was if Heaven could feel his pain.

"Robbie, what the hell are you doing out here, you had me and your mother worried sick," his father's voice was rough, but soft, almost tired.

Suddenly time caught up with him, it was like being hit in the ass by a rubber band that had been stretched until it seemed it would snap being released.

"I... I don't know," he said breathlessly, he realized his whole body was drenched. By rain or by sweat, he wasn't sure.

"My God, you're freezing! Get in the car before you catch cold!" his mother pulled him up and led him to the car. He saw police lights and it took him a moment to focus on the police car parked next to his parents'. Now he knew where the sirens had been coming from.

He heard his mother gasp, "What did you do to your hand?" he looked down at it, hanging limply by his side, blood running down his fingertips and staining his pants.

"I, uh..." he didn't know how she'd react to him saying he hit the gravestone of someone he didn't even know, "I'm not sure..."

His mother took the scarf from around her neck and wrapped it around his hand and his father gave him his bomber jacket.

His mother practically shoved him in the car and he saw an exchange between his parents and the police. Then his parents climbed in the car and everyone was silent the whole way home.

October 21, 2010

Robbie was standing right outside of Mr. Danver's classroom, watching Lydia's locker. He wanted to talk to her; he'd been missing her terribly. He saw her heading to her locker. But that wasn't what made anger begin bubbling up inside him. Calvin Stevenson was walking behind her, carrying her books and listening to what she was saying intently. Once they stopped at the locker, they just stood there, talking. When

58

Lydia smiled at him, Robbie felt as if a razor blade were making its way through his digestive tract. He turned away; he couldn't bear to watch them any longer. He walked away, without saying a word to her.

When he got home, he sat down in his room. He sat, glaring at his reflection in his computer screen for the longest time. Then, suddenly he sprang up and swung his arm at his bookshelf, causing it to fall, spilling its contents onto the floor.

He heard someone running up the stairs; his mother no doubt. And alas, there she was, standing in the doorway, staring wide-eyed into his room.

"What the hell is going on up here?" she yelled; she was apparently very angry, it wasn't often that Mrs. Pierce cursed. He stared blankly at the books and knick-knacks scattered about his floor, "I don't know what is wrong with you, Robbie, but I'm sure it's more than some survivor's guilt. You need to go back to Dr. Wilder," she shook her head and started to leave the room.

"I'm not going back to her."

"And why not?"

"It'd be a waste of your money."

"Well then how am I supposed to help you, Robbie? Huh? Please, tell me what the hell I'm supposed to do!"

"Leave me alone! Just-" he threw himself on his bed and grabbed his hair, balling his hands into fists, "Stop treating me like there's something wrong with me."

"But there is something wrong with you!"

"I was with Ryan when he died! I may not remember the exact moment, but I was there, next to him, dying! My heart stopped, Mom, my heart stopped! I shoulda died, but here I am, having to deal with everyone's bullshit about how I'm not happy. Why the hell would I be happy, there's nothing to be happy about! I've lost everything, I've lost my brother, my friends, my family's opinion of my sanity, Lydia... and I'm sick of it! I'm sick of all of it! I feel so alone, even when people try to make things better, it's like they're miles away. It's like I'm dead to the world, so please, let me sort this out all by myself! You think I've got a problem? Well, I wonder why I'd have one," he was tense all over, breathing hard.

His mother was crying now, "I already lost one son, Robbie, I couldn't bear to lose another, especially when you're the only other son I have. But it's as if I've lost you already. I just... I just... I just want my son back."

He covered his face with his hands and let out a loud sigh. She slid down the wall, sobbing silently.

He glanced at her between his fingers. They stayed like this for what seemed like hours but in reality was probably only a couple of minutes.

She suddenly felt his hand on her shoulder. She looked up and saw him standing over her. He took her hands and helped her up. Then, he walked over to his fallen shelf and stood it up. He began to pick things up off the floor.

"Sorry," he said quietly, not looking at her.

"Robbie, I-"

"Please leave."

She stood there a moment, her mouth still open to speak. Then she closed it and went back downstairs.

He picked up a broken picture frame and looked at the photograph in it. It was Ryan and himself, sitting in the bed of his brand new truck.

October 26, 2010

Five days. Five days now he had watched Lydia and Calvin, acting like the best of friends when they had barely known each other a mere month before. He didn't know why it made him feel so sick to see her with him; it wasn't like they were engaged, or even together for that matter. He finally got the guts to get up and walk over to where they were sitting.

"Lydia, can we talk?" he said; he thought his voice sounded strange, strained.

"I guess," she looked really uncomfortable.

"Everything alright?" Calvin asked, eyeing Robbie like one buck may eye another before ramming its head into it.

"Yeah, it'll only take a second," she stood and walked to the window with Robbie, "What?"

"You said you needed time to sort things out. Well?"

"I don't know, Robbie, have *you* sorted things out yet?"

He opened his mouth to speak, but his voice caught in his throat. He struggled to get some words out, "Lydia, all I know is I love you and I need you right now."

She looked hurt for a moment before saying, "Robbie, I think time away is best, just some time away."

She returned to where Calvin was sitting and said something to him and he glared in Robbie's direction.

October 31, 2010

Halloween had been Robbie's favorite holiday. However now, as he looked out his bedroom window at all the trick-or-treaters dressed as skeletons and ghosts, it just didn't seem as fun. Maybe it was because he'd been seeing dead people, real dead people, not white sheets and printed silhouettes of glow in the dark bones.

He left his window; he'd seen enough ghosts and death figures.

He lay down on his bed and soon was asleep.

Bright light shined in his eyes. He put his hand up to shield himself, squinting. Soon he realized he was by the caves. He felt drawn to a certain cave; the same one Ryan had led him to. He walked in and looked around. His eyes stopped on a figure dressed all in black, its back to him. He realized it was Marcy.

He approached her; she didn't seem to notice him. He looked at her face; she was staring at the ground, silent tears running down her cheeks. He remembered the shadow, it was here, this was where they'd found Marcy's body. This must have been where she was raped and murdered.

He took in a breath to say something her, but then she spoke, ever so quietly and distant, "It's hard to stand there... the place you died. All those feelings just come back to you: the fear, the adrenaline rush, struggling for air... and that doom you feel inside you when you know you're going to die," she wiped her cheek with the palm of her hand, "Try it; try standing in the place where you died. You'll understand what I mean," she looked up at him, "It's more painful than anything you can imagine."

"This is where you died."

She nodded.

"Why... why can I see you?"

"We share something, you and I," she smiled a weak sideways smile; he had never taken much notice to how beautiful she was but her smile made it impossible to overlook.

"What?"

She shook her head and looked around the cave. As she did, he could see bruises welling up on her neck and her lips turning blue.

"I can usually hide it in your head," she said, "But not here."

"Hide what?"

"What I look like. Ryan looks like he did in the accident because he shows himself in your everyday life. Here I have some control over what you can and can't see."

"Marcy, who killed you?"

"I... I don't remember. That's why I came back here. I can remember his face... but it's distorted, he looks like a demon in my memories and the name is completely gone... I suppose that's because he *is* a demon to me," she sniffed and swallowed, trying to stop the crying.

Robbie stood there, feeling helpless; he wanted to comfort her, but he kept reminding himself she was dead.

"Every time I think about him, I see that demon and then... and then I feel drawn to you. From the moment I died, the first person I saw was Ryan. And he led me to you. And since then, it's like I'm drawn to you. I've no idea what fate has in store for us... but there seems to be no other reason for this but fate," she hugged him, leaning her head against his chest, "You're cold... yet you're oddly warm. How strange it is to hear a beating heart and feel the rise and fall of someone's breathing."

He patted her back, "Is this lonely... is being a ghost like a dream you can't wake up from?"

"I guess that's how you could put it."

"The place I feel the most at home is a cemetery... and the people I have conversations with that mean something are dead."

"There's a reason for that."

"What?"

He was back in his room, embracing a blanket. Nothing more. He could feel places on his face where tears had dried.

November

November 2, 2010

Robbie pulled over to the shoulder of the road. He knew this spot, the curve in the road was unmistakable. He climbed out of the truck and walked over to the spot where the cow had been standing. He looked out over the soybean field and saw a patch where the plants looked wilted and crushed, he knew that was where the car must have been laying.

He walked out into the field to that spot and as he stepped onto the wilted patch of crops, he felt a deep sadness in himself, as if he'd been enveloped in a shell of ice. He winced and thought back to that day; so happy and carefree he'd been... Ryan had been too. And then he'd died. Death does that to you, it sneaks up on you when you're not ready for it, when you're not prepared to fight it off.

He felt an icy cold hand on his shoulder and his eyes flew open. He looked up and saw Ryan standing beside him, looking at him with the same sadness in his eyes Marcy had had in his dream. They stared at each other in a strange silence. It was surreal, for them to both to be back in the place where Ryan had died and Robbie nearly had.

"It's been two months..." Robbie said quietly, unable to look away from Ryan's bruised face. He slowly nodded, looking down at the patch of ground where his car had been totaled and where he had been crushed to death. Tears gleamed in his bloodshot eyes and slid down his purple/black cheeks. He closed his eyes as if deep in thought and slowly faded away.

Robbie could still feel his icy fingers on his arm, even though he wasn't there anymore, "Two months..." he said quietly, "Two months since everything changed."

He tried so hard to remember what'd been running through his mind those last few moments before they'd rounded the bend. What had he been thinking, not knowing of the doom that awaited them only a few seconds ahead. But he just couldn't remember. It was as if those thoughts had been purged from his mind, they no longer seemed to exist or matter.

He walked back to his truck. A gust of wind blew across the open country. It sounded almost as if it were calling him, airy and whispering "Robbie..."

He turned over his shoulder to look over the soybean field once more before climbing into his truck and driving away.

November 5, 2010

"Cal, you are too funny!" Lydia laughed, twirling her fork in her cafeteria spaghetti, but not eating any.

"Well, what can I say, that's how it happened," he smiled across the table at her. He was a handsome young man with neatly combed black hair and stubble that somehow looked sophisticated on his face. He had gleaming hazel eyes and perfect white teeth that made his smile simply astonishing. You never caught him without a button up shirt and nice slacks accompanied by Dockers. He was like a businessman with a teenage edge.

"Well, I'm sorry, but I gotta go. Have a meeting with the principal," he raised his eyebrows, "See you after school," he flashed his signature smile, and then picked up the small briefcase he kept all his papers in and left the cafeteria.

"What's up with you and Cal?" Sam asked, coming over and sitting down where Calvin had been sitting a few seconds before.

"We just kinda started talking. I'm glad we did though, we have a lot in common and-" she paused and stared out the window, staring off into space, "he makes me smile," she said quietly.

"Does Robbie know?"

"I don't know... I think he has some idea."

"Most people are saying they heard you broke up. I guess people spread things around, seeing as you two haven't been too friendly with each other."

"I," she closed her eyes, trying not to cry, "I miss Robbie... I miss *my* Robbie."

He scooted his chair closer to her and put his arm around her, "He doesn't mean to hurt you... he hasn't meant to hurt anyone, I don't think. He's just... having a rough time."

"I know, it's just," she stopped; she didn't want to tell Sam about the cave incident, "Nothing."

He stifled a laugh, "It's always something... especially when you say it's nothing."

"Yeah," she was quiet a moment, "Don't say anything about me and Cal... to anyone, we're just friends."

"I won't."

After school, Lydia stood outside, waiting for Calvin. He didn't show. The parking lot was practically empty when she saw his friend, Devin. Devin said Calvin had gone home sick; he'd been throwing up almost uncontrollably when he got to the principal's office. She looked around and saw Robbie in his truck, staring at her. He looked away when her gaze met his and pulled out of the parking lot.

November 6, 2010

Mr. Pierce sensed a presence in the entrance to the den; it was Robbie.

"Wanna come in?" he asked, rather surprised; Robbie usually stayed in his room when he was home.

He slowly walked in and sat down on the sofa. He looked up at the ceiling fan and his father looked at him.

"Dad, can I talk to you about something?"

"Of course, son."

"Why do girls do it? They play with your heart; one minute they act like they love you, the next they hate you, and the next they don't even seem to know."

"Problems with Lydia?" he asked, taking off his glasses.

"... yeah."

"Well, girls are weird in that way. Take your mother, for example, we had our fights and she seemed to hate me for a time, but look at us now," he went to the small fridge in the corner of the den and pulled out a Miller and a Coke.

"I don't want anything," Robbie said. His father put the Coke back in the fridge.

"So, what I'm saying, son," his father grunted, trying to open the Miller, "is that girls are confusing, they seldom show what they really want. But go for it. Be persistent. Who knows, you and Lydia may end up like me and your mother one day."

Robbie blew his breath; maybe it was a strained laugh, "I highly doubt that... she won't talk to me and has been avoiding me for weeks now."

Mr. Pierce shrugged, "You never know, maybe she's acting that way to see if you're really serious; to see if you'll follow her as she runs," he chuckled, sipping his beer.

Robbie shook his head, "I don't know..." he stared up at the fan again, watching it spin. Then he stood and left the den quietly. He stopped in the doorway, "Thanks, Dad."

November 10, 2010

"So, I heard Cal has the stomach flu," Sam said across the table to Lydia, slurping down his blue Jell-O.

"Oh," she stared out the window; it was storming.

"I haven't talked to Robbie lately; have you?" he asked.

"No."

"Ah. I see him, we just haven't really talked since his party."

"Every time I see him, he's staring at me, but once he sees me looking, he looks away."

"He misses you," Sam shrugged, putting the last of his Jell-O in his mouth.

November 12, 2010

Instant Messenger (9:23 P.M.)

Calvin Stevenson: hey, i think i maybe getting better, would you wanna hang out sometime soon?
Lydia Farmer: hm... like, when?
Calvin Stevenson: idk, 20th, 21st... 22nd?
Lydia Farmer: 21st would b good :)
Calvin Stevenson: yay

Lydia Farmer: lol

Calvin Stevenson: the flu really sucks, i've missed like three tests

Lydia Farmer: ugh, makeup work sux

Calvin Stevenson: I know, right? :)

Lydia Farmer: so, whatta u wanna do the 21st?

Calvin Stevenson: its a surprise ;)

Lydia Farmer: haha, ok *nervous*

Calvin Stevenson: why you nervous, lol?

Lydia Farmer: maybe not nervous, anxious :) lol

Calvin Stevenson: guess youll just have to wait til the 21st :p
btw, where do you live?

Lydia Farmer: 9210 Maple Drive

Calvin Stevenson: k, thanks, gotta know where to pick you up ;) lol

Lydia Farmer: yepyep

Calvin Stevenson: well, off to bed, gotta sleep if I wanna get better :) byez ♥

Calvin Stevenson is offline.

November 16, 2010

Robbie could hear his cell phone going off. It'd been forever since anyone had called him and his Coldplay ringtone sounded very unfamiliar.

"Hey man," it was Sam, "What's up?"

"Nothing."

"Oh... you wanna hang out?"

"Not necessarily."

He heard Sam sigh on the other end.

"What do you wanna do?" he asked, even though he couldn't be less interested.

"I dunno. Go see a movie. Screw around at the arcade. Paintball," he could hear mischief in Sam's voice on that last one.

"What movies are showing?"

"There's a pretty epic comedy all the guys have been seeing."

"Sure, whatever, we can see that," Robbie said.

"Awesome. Six thirty?"

"Sure."

"Alright! Bye!"

Robbie sat through the whole movie with Sam laughing stupidly at the terrible jokes. Robbie just thought it was the most ridiculous thing he'd ever seen, though when Sam asked him what he thought, he said it was funny.

November 19, 2010

"Hey, you wanna hang out the day after tomorrow?" Sam asked Lydia, picking at his chicken stir fry; he didn't trust all cafeteria food.

"I'd like to, but I already have plans with Cal."

"Isn't he still sick?"

"He thinks he's getting better."

"Oh, that's good. So, what're you two gonna do?"

"I don't know; he said it's a surprise."

"Oh," Sam shifted uncomfortably before getting up and disposing of his stir fry.

November 20, 2010

Robbie was laying on the den sofa, watching the ceiling fan spin. He watched it repeat the same motion again and again and again. He was snapped out of his hypnotism by an incoming text message. He flipped open his phone and read it.

It was from Sam, "hey man, lydia is going out with Cal Stevenson 2morow".

He felt razorblades in his intestines again. He replied, "oh."

"arent u 2 still 2gether?"

"idk"

"oh..."

Robbie stopped replying after that.

November 21, 2010

"Hello," Calvin said smiling that signature smile of his as Lydia met him at the side door; she didn't want her father having a cow over 'a new one.'

He was dressed as snazzy as usual, even more so due to the violet and black striped tie he was wearing. She was wearing a nice blouse and black skinny jeans.

He led her to his car, "I'm going to have to blindfold you."

"Why?" she looked uncomfortable for a moment.

"Don't wanna spoil the surprise," he smiled, tying a bandana around her head.

Suddenly, Robbie's eyes flew open. He'd been laying on his bed, resting, but not sleeping. He had a sudden feeling, a bad feeling. He picked up his phone and called the Farmers.

Mr. Farmer answered, "Hello?"

"Can I speak to Lydia?"

"She don't wanna talk to you," he growled.

"Listen, please, it's import-" he heard Mr. Farmer hang up.

"Shit!" he yelled and had to keep himself from flinging his phone across the room. He took some deep breaths to calm himself down. He dialed Lydia's cell phone. It rang and went to her voicemail. He hung up. He stood, leaning against his room's doorframe for a minute.

Then he called again. And once again, he got her voicemail, "Lydia, I know you don't wanna talk to me, but this is important, please, don't go out anywhere tonight, just stay home... please, stay home!" he hung up and threw his phone on his bed.

He sat in his computer chair and laid his head in his hands, grabbing his hair in frustration.

"Voila," Calvin said, removing the blindfold and led Lydia into a cave lit by candlelight and the cutest little picnic.

"Aw, Cal," Lydia was taken aback; this had to be the best dinner she'd been to in a while.

"Sit," he said, sitting down on one side of the blanket.

Lydia looked around and suddenly realized it was the cave where she and Robbie had had their fight. She didn't bother Calvin with that though.

"What's wrong?" he asked seriously, looking at her face.

"Thinking about Robbie..."

"Poor guy," he said, beginning to butter a piece of bread, "He lost his brother in a car accident, right?"

"Yeah."

"That's sad... but still no excuse for the way he treated you."

"Yeah... I just don't know what happened to him. He really... he really changed after that."

"Sorry."

"Don't worry about it," she grabbed an apple abruptly, wanting to change the subject.

<u>November 22, 2010</u>

"Dammit! Dammit! Why!?" Robbie couldn't kill the feeling in his gut, he *needed* to talk to Lydia. He climbed in his truck and took off; he didn't know where he was going, but recently, when had that mattered.

"So, when is your birthday?" Calvin asked.

"In February. February sixteenth."

"Ah," he loosened his tie, "I'm gonna be nineteen in a few weeks."

"What!? There is no way you flunked a grade."

"No," he chuckled, "My mom started me in school a year late. Don't ask me why, she just did."

"Okay," she laughed.

His face turned serious, "Lydia, do you like me?"

"Well, yeah, you're a really good friend and all-"

"I wanna be more than just friends."

"Cal, I don't know," she turned away, trying to hide her tears; she still wasn't completely over Robbie.

Suddenly, she saw something fly over her head and felt a rope tightening around her throat. She whipped around to see Calvin grinning maliciously at her, an end of his tie in each hand, "I wanna be *much* more than just friends."

"Cal, stop, what are you doing!?" she tried to scream, but it was a choked whisper.

"Be a good girl, Lydia, screaming won't do you any good out here anyway. That's why I chose it," his smile widened as he pulled his tie tighter around her neck.

And suddenly she remembered the Bivens case. Nobody had known who Marcy was out with that night and nobody knew who she was with. She felt the tie slacken, but she was too weak to fight back. She heard him rip something; it sounded like paper. And then she heard him unzipping his pants.

Suddenly two hands grabbed Calvin by the collar, pulling him off of Lydia and throwing him against the wall. Calvin found himself face to face with Robbie Pierce, his eyes burning with a fire like Hell.

"You get away from her!" Robbie yelled through gritted teeth, hitting him against the wall.

"Get away from *me* you freak," Calvin yelled, shoving Robbie back. He fell backwards, but his grip on Calvin's shirt did not slacken, so he brought him down with him, "You son of a bitch," Calvin shoved his knee up between Robbie's legs and he cried out, clutching his crotch.

Calvin stood and began to walk back towards Lydia. She had begun crawling out of the cave; the first light of dawn was shining over the trees. Suddenly Calvin felt someone pounce on his back; how had Robbie recovered from that blow so quickly?

They both went tumbling down the small slope outside the cave and hit a tree. Calvin cried out in pain. Robbie grabbed his collar with one hand and drew his other back in a fist. Calvin saw the scars on his knuckles right before they came in contact with his perfect face. Robbie drew back and hit him again. He felt his knuckles splitting again; Calvin felt one of his perfect teeth being knocked loose.

Robbie was about to hit him again, but gained control of himself. Calvin was out cold anyway. He thought of Lydia in the cave. He stood and ran towards her.

"Lydia," he cried out and he saw her sitting in the entrance to the cave, crying. Suddenly he felt dizzy. He began to stumble from side to side. The sky seemed bright, too bright for this time of morning. The best thing he could compare it to was when he'd gotten drunk on his sixteenth birthday.

He fell to his knees, "Lydia..." everything was spinning. He saw Lydia looking in his direction, trying to stop the crying, her mouth agape. He saw Marcy and Ryan flanking the entrance to the cave. He fell on his back. He was breathing quick shallow breaths. He could hear his heart beating in his temples.

He felt a cold hand on his shoulder and looked up to see Ryan stooped over him, his mouth in a tight line but he thought he saw the curves of a smile at the edges. There was a certain pity in his eyes. He looked to his other side and saw Marcy, fighting tears, but smiling her beautiful smile. He saw Ryan's smile widen and a slight nod and then everything grew silent. And still. And black.

Lydia rushed to his side, "Robbie! Robbie! Robbie!" she was screaming his name, "Oh God, Robbie, please," she took a deep breath; she needed to regain her head. She pulled out her cell phone and dialed 911. Soon she heard sirens and the police and ambulances arrived. Calvin was loaded into an ambulance and taken to the hospital.

Some medics came to examine Robbie; Lydia had his head cradled on her lap and she was stroking his hair. She saw them put a stethoscope to his chest and the seconds they listened seemed like decades. The one listening lifted his head and looked at the other medic seriously before shaking his head. Lydia burst into tears as they brought a defibrillator from the ambulance and tried to restart his heart. Every time they shocked him, they'd listen and the same head shake would follow.

She saw the Pierces' car pull up and Mrs. Pierce trying to run over, the police stopping her, Mr. Pierce taking her in his arms, her crying into his chest.

Robbie was pronounced dead at the scene. What the coroner didn't tell them was that tests run to determine the time of death showed he'd been dead for several months. The Pierces took Lydia home, where she was greeted and hugged and kissed by her tearful parents. Lydia called Sam and he cried harder than most guys would admit they cried. He told Alex and he took his rifle and went out into the woods; he returned several hours later with five fat squirrels, but he had no pride in them this time. Ms. Moscow promised her sister to come down at once.

It rained that day; it was as if the heavens knew of the great sacrifice made that day and was crying just the same as everyone.

November 26, 2010

A knock came at the Pierces' door. Mrs. Pierce answered it and saw Lydia standing there; she was wearing a black dress.

"Can I talk to you, Mrs. Pierce?"

"Of course, dear, come in, have some tea."

Lydia sat down on the sofa and Mrs. Pierce sat in the leather recliner.

Lydia took in air to say something, but her voice seemed to be stuck in her throat, "Robbie," she struggled to get his name out, "Robbie saved my life. If he hadn't showed up, I would be dead right now. I don't know how he knew where I was; it's a miracle I'm here right now, Mrs. Pierce."

She saw tears gleaming in Mrs. Pierce's eyes, "You were his world. He would've given anything for you. He... the fact he lived through that car crash was a miracle," she stared out the window distantly.

"I loved him... I just, got confused and befuddled and I... I abandoned him. And he still came through for me," silent tears slid down her cheeks, causing her eye liner to run, "In the end, he was there for me... he was my Robbie again," she stood and wiped her eyes, "Mrs. Pierce, you had a very... amazing son and I'm going to miss him as long as I live," she bent down and kissed the top of Mrs. Pierce's head before leaving.

Ryan Alexander Pierce
December 14, 1990 -September 2,
2010

Marcy Bivens
"only the good die young"
March 12, 1991 - September
2, 2010

Robert Justin Pierce
October 8, 1992 - November 22, 2010

...

Robert Justin Pierce
October 8, 1992 - September 2, 2010

December

December 3, 2010

Lydia sat down on Robbie's bed. The room seemed drafty. Cold. Empty. Fluffy white snowflakes fell serenely outside the window. As cold and empty as the room felt, it was peaceful in a way.

She stood and walked over to his desk. His parents had told her she could have photographs of her and Robbie. She began to go through a pile of papers by his computer. Not too deep into the pile she found an envelope. It was addressed 'To Whom It May Concern'.

She took the envelope and sat back down on the bed. She opened it and saw Robbie's handwriting; the handwriting she'd seen in his first love note to her.

"Ever since the accident, when Ryan died, nothing has been the same. I have been completely alone. Nobody can understand what I feel inside; I myself do not understand it. It is a feeling of... emptiness. Loneliness. It's like a bad dream I can't wake up from. I realize everyone is trying to help and I appreciate it, but it just frustrates me because I don't know how to talk about it. Lydia was the one who came closest to understanding, but still she seemed miles away most of the time... and now I have lost her too. I didn't used to cry much, but now I feel like I do a lot. It has been since I met Marcy Bivens, she has changed my life... I feel a strange bond with her and I feel it is her I cry for when everyone thinks I'm crying for Ryan. Not that I don't cry for him, but I can feel the sadness emanate from her when I am with her. I don't understand a lot of things, after all, I am only eighteen, but even the elders in my life don't seem to have experienced what I am going through and they say wisdom comes with life experience. I wonder how many of them have died... how many of those people who tell you that you couldn't understand yet, have died? They say I wasn't dead, that my heart just stopped, but is it not the same thing? Death is a very inconceivable thing. It is dark and lonely and cold. We don't talk about it much because it makes us uncomfortable; we try to run and hide from it. It's a very scary concept, to not be anymore. Because as much as we say we believe in God or an afterlife, we don't really know what happens after death. They say ghosts stay bound to the Earth because of unfinished business. I can only imagine the feeling of being stuck in a world where no one can see you trying to solve a task when you have no idea what it is. For I have seen them; I have seen their pain, though I have no idea to what degree it must hurt. But I can fathom what it feels like, to be so alone when surrounded by so many people. I feel this way every day. As everyone reaches out, their arms don't reach, they're far too short to reach me where I am perched and only God knows where exactly that is.

According to Marcy, I am here for a reason, there was a reason that they could 'bring me back'. I hope I can discover what that is, perhaps then I can get my life back. Perhaps once I finish my 'unfinished business', I can move on from this stage of life, into the next.

A strange thought has passed through my mind recently. Considering that I am alive, and yet I feel dead to the world, could perhaps those that are dead to the world still be alive? Perhaps death and life are one thing, merely different stages. We are born and then grow to be toddlers and then to be children and then we hit adolescence and become teenagers and before we know it we are adults and then the white hairs and wrinkles and joint problems begin. And then we die. Could death just be the stage after becoming old? Where do we go after we die? Marcy and Ryan and God knows how many others are stuck in the ghost stage of their life. Because they are still there;

they are still conscious. They haven't survived death. Where they will go when they move on, I don't know. But now they are here, like us, living every day alone surrounded by people. Have you ever been in a room surrounded by people and yet felt you were completely alone? That is the best way to convey what death feels like to someone who is still in the mainstream stage of life. If zombies were real, that would be how I would describe my life. I exist and therefore I am. But *what* am I? I do not know and I don't think Dr. Wilder could have answered that question. If you happen to be reading this, my guess is I am dead now. Perhaps no one will ever read this, perhaps it will be thrown away with all my old school papers, who knows? But this is a chapter of my life, and Mom, Dad, Lydia, Sam, Alex, or whoever is reading this, I want to end it by saying I love you. No matter how I've treated you or what I've said to you, I love you.

Robbie Pierce"

She was crying, yet she was smiling. He seemed so confused, so lost, it was heartbreaking. But he had ended it with the three most meaningful words one person can say to another.

Lydia looked out the window at the small pieces of white fluff, slowly falling from the heavens. Each one unique and beautiful, yet sooner or later it would hit the ground and be lost forever in the others. Then it would melt, but its memory would live on in the plants that thrived from the moisture it'd provided.

Watching the snow fall, Lydia knew Robbie had moved onto this next stage, he was at peace; he was no longer lost and alone. And he would never be forgotten. She sat the paper on the window sill, turned, and walked out of Robbie Pierce's room for the last time.

And to Close
(an author's note)

If you do not understand what you have read, Robbie Pierce died with his brother, Ryan Pierce. However, he was bound to this earth by one thing: his love for Lydia. As fate would have it he also shared a death date with Marcy Bivens, the first of Calvin Stevenson's rape/murder victims. Because of the reason he was still bound to his body, with an even stronger bond than a ghost. Once Robbie's 'unfinished business' was resolved, he was allowed to pass on. This is why the coroner's test showed he'd been dead for several months; his spirit had been keeping a dead husk alive but not truly alive.

Keep in mind Robbie Pierce did not know he was dead, he only thought perhaps he had been dead for those two cold minutes. The significance of the number two is represented several places in this book: Ryan Pierce and Marcy Bivens, two people, died on September second. Robbie Pierce's heart stopped for two minutes. Lydia Farmer was Calvin Stevenson's second victim. And Robbie 'died' on November twenty-second.

I hope you enjoyed this tale of life and death with an underlying love story. It makes me think of the quote "True love never dies."

About the Author

Sarah J Dhue lives in Illinois with her family. She began writing at a very young age. As well as writing, Sarah is a photographer, graphic designer, art enthusiast, and animal lover. She first wrote 'For Two Cold Minutes' when she was sixteen and it was her first fill length novella. Its first printing was in May 2012 by Lynn's Printing.